THIS **Elephant & Piggie** BOOK
BELONGS TO:

_____

_____

_____

To Megan Alrutz
for listening to my long, crazy stories

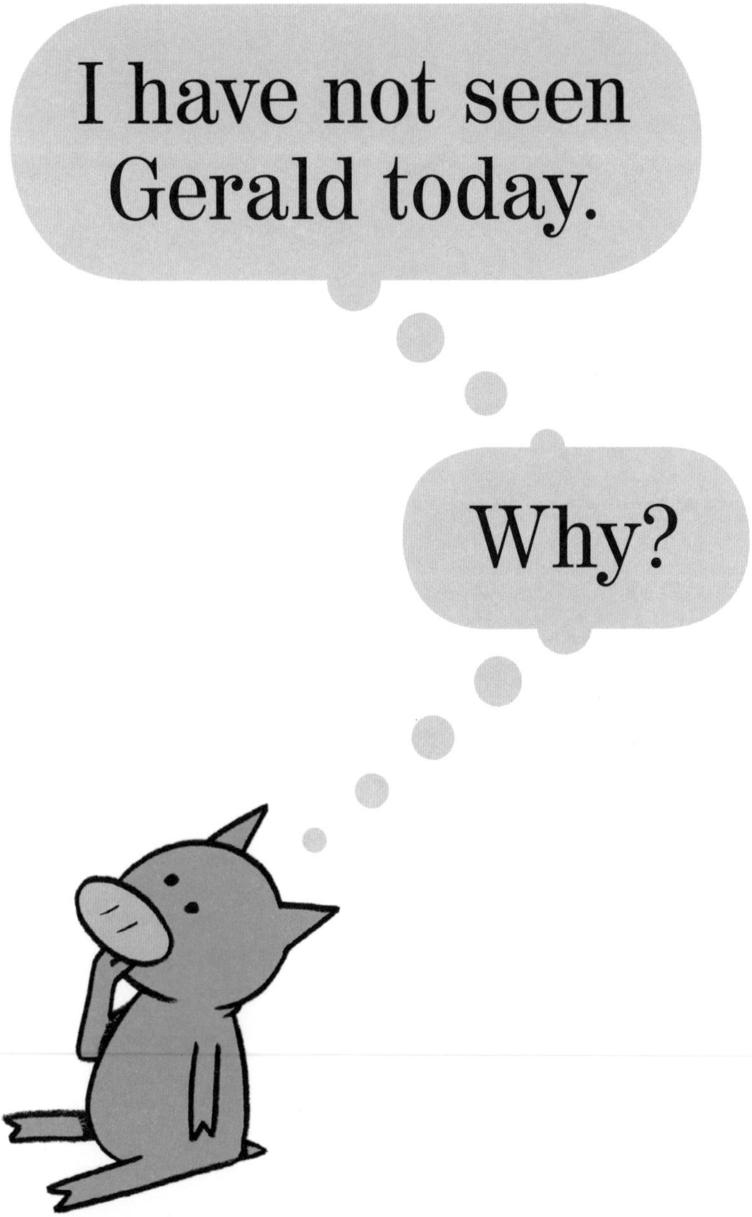
I have not seen Gerald today.
Why?

4

9

Well...

I was playing with Hippo.

Then, I had an idea!
I wanted to lift Hippo
onto my trunk!

There is more
to my story.

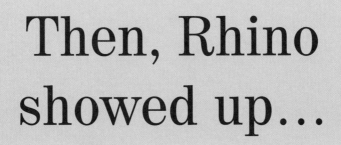

Rhino wanted a turn.

What did
you do?

But a hippo *and* a rhino on your trunk are very heavy.

29

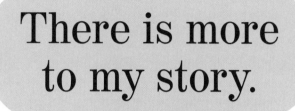

There is more
to my story.

37

41

This *is* a long, crazy story...

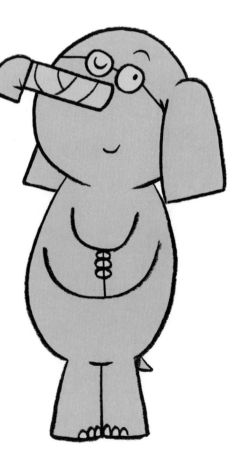

45

Well, I was so proud
of what I had done …

that I ran to tell my very best friend about it!

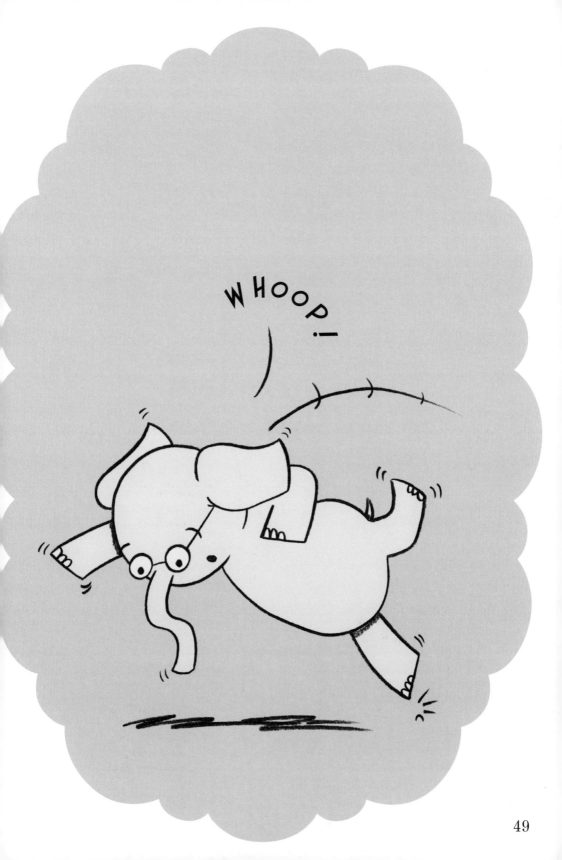

49

51

That is a *funny* story!

WHOOP.

55

Piggie!

What happened to your snout?

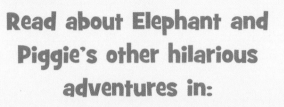

Read about Elephant and Piggie's other hilarious adventures in: